The Shoes

Written by

Dr. Ruth M. Wilson

BK
ROYSTON
Publishing

BK Royston Publishing
Jeffersonville, IN 47131
http://www.bkroystonpublishing.com
bkroystonpublishing@gmail.com

Cover Design: Johnathan Johnson, Merge Media

ISBN-13: 978-1-967282-56-2

Printed in the United States of America

Dedication

This book is dedicated to shoe designers all over the world, you know who you are, and to every woman upon this earth who loves shoes.

Table of Contents

Introduction

Being questioned by homicide detective Brian Johnson, there were two questions that were asked of everyone on the floor of our luxury apartment. "Did you see or hear anything?" Upon questioning me, I was able to give him an answer due to the fact that this strange woman was making her exit as I was coming down the hall. All I could tell him, however, was that she was tall, dressed in all black from head to toe, but it was the shoes that she wore that stood out for me. I had never seen shoes like that before.

They had to have been created by a well-known shoe designer—four-inch heels, covered in diamonds.

I guess he was wondering how I could tell they were diamonds instead of rhinestones. My answer to him before he could ask the question was, "Because rhinestones don't shine like that. Plus, the sister was stepping like she was on the runway for Couture Fashion Week."

Chapter 1

Dressed for Fashion Week

I was returning home from another wonderful breakfast at Holy Belly this morning. I had decided to treat myself after receiving a big promotion at my job, from the administrative staff in the coroner's office to the position of full-time pathologist, specializing in lab and tissue analysis and others in cadavers/autopsies.

As I stepped off the elevator, a woman was approaching me dressed in all black. Not recognizing her, my first thought was that maybe she was a client of Alex's, a well-known attorney who lived on our floor, or maybe she was the new resident whom I had yet to meet.

Whoever she was, she was sharp from head to toe, starting with the large black hat she had on down to those shoes.

I had never seen shoes like those before, except on a runway.

Wherever she was going, she was definitely going to be the sharpest person there.

As I continued to my apartment, from around the corner, I could hear someone screaming.

Turning the corner, I saw that it was Maria, the housekeeper. She was screaming because she had found Evening dead; she had been murdered.

Evening was the owner of one of the largest jewelry stores in Paris.

Who could have done this? Everyone loved and respected Evening. Was it robbery, a jealous lover? *Who could have done this?* Again, I wondered, who could have done this to her and why.

The police were called by several people after hearing Maria scream. Many residents were running out of their apartments to see what was happening.

As the detectives began to investigate, there were two questions that were asked of everyone.

"Did you see anything?"

"Did you hear anything?"

Everyone on our floor who was home was questioned by the homicide detectives.

When it was my turn, Detective Brian Johnson talked to me.

I was able to give him an answer, due to the fact that a woman I had never seen in our building before was making her exit as I was coming down the hall.

All I could tell him was she was tall, dressed in all black, except for the shoes.

I told him I had never seen shoes like that before. They had to have been created by a well-known designer.

They were four-inch heels, covered with diamonds.

"Diamonds?" he repeated.

"Yes, diamonds, not rhinestones, not cubic zirconia, diamonds!"

I guess he was wondering how I could tell that they were diamonds.

My answer to him before he could ask the question was, "Because rhinestones don't shine like that. The sister was stepping like she was a model on the runway in Couture Fashion Week."

"Could you tell what race or nationality she was?" he asked.

"No, because the hat she was wearing covered her face; plus, she had on dark glasses."

"Thank you; if you remember anything else," he said, handing me his card, "please feel free to give me a call."

When I got to work that afternoon, lying on the examiner's table was

Evening Zamora, my neighbor who was murdered. My curiosity immediately set in.

I asked Coroner Jacobs if he had determined the cause of death yet.

His answer was, "Yes. Poison!"

"Poison?" I asked?

"Yes, it was put in her drink," he explained.

"What was the drink?" I wanted to know.

"Coffee."

"What kind of poison was it?" I asked, wanting to know as much as I could.

"Fentanyl!" the doctor said.

"Fentanyl?" I asked, surprised.

"Yes, fentanyl," he repeated.

I knew that fentanyl was fifty times more potent than heroin and one-hundred times more potent than morphine.

He told me that in 2020, in the United States alone, 117,045 people overdosed from fentanyl.

"Wow!" was all I could say, knowing that Evening never indulged in any type of drugs or alcohol.

At this point, my mind was spinning, desperately trying to figure this one out.

Because Evening had a heart of gold, she would help anybody. I just couldn't imagine who would want to kill her.

That told me that this woman had to have known her personally or she was a delivery person, because our apartment complex was secured. A person had to be buzzed in by the resident; plus, there was security at the front desk.

In being my investigative self, I was determined to get to the bottom of the mystery of who that woman was, and why she felt the need to kill Evening.

Chapter 2

L'As du Fallafel at 44

Looking at Evening lying on the table, for some odd reason, I decided to pull the sheet all the way off her. In doing so, to my surprise, I saw that she had on the same shoes the woman in black was wearing.

That told me that this was personal.

Who could have done this? Was it her business partner or someone else?

Now, inquiring minds really wanted to know.

I decided to reach out to detective Brian Johnson to see what he knew. I invited him to lunch.

We planned to meet at L'As du Fallafel at 44, rue des Rosiers, one of my favorite places to have lunch.

Sitting across the table staring into Mr. Johnson's eye, intently listening and grabbing ahold of every word that was coming off those sweet sexy lips of his, I had to snatch myself back. That man was handsome!

He shared with me that the first thing he noticed was the shoes that Evening had on. Then, me sharing with him that the woman who got on the elevator was wearing the same shoes, raised suspicion for the both of us.

All I could think of was, *those were $10,000.00 shoes!*

To my shock, he was sharing with me that his wife has those same shoes. Not knowing the cost, he never questioned her about them. I was not willing to tell him how much they were really worth if she had the real deal.

All I could think about was, *there goes my opportunity to have a date; he's married!* Oh well, it was about who killed my friend Evening anyhow.

While we were eating, Detective Brian received a call telling him to get to a parking garage right away, Parking Saemes - Rivoli Sébastopol, 5 r Pernelle. There had been another murder.

I asked him if I could accompany him, to which he agreed, since our lunch was cut short and I was a pathologist in the coroner's office.

Off we went, blue lights, siren, at fast speed, with me holding on for dear life trying to hold on to my drink without spilling it. When we arrived, the police were everywhere. The garage was covered from top to bottom, to make sure if the murderer was still in the garage, he or she would be found.

As we walked up to the car, we could see that the victim was lying across the front seat. I could tell that there had been a struggle. She had been strangled. The handprints on her neck were visible.

"Oh, not again," we both said at the same time. "not the same shoes." Only, this time, they were red in color, and the diamonds were circled.

What is it about these shoes? I wondered. We both wondered.

Two murders in two days. What in the world was going on?

Whatever it was, it was tied to the shoes. It had to be!

As detective Brian began to question the woman who dialed 17 for the police, she, Frances Baldwin, told him that upon entering the garage, she heard a struggle and screams and then it got quiet.

She said she quickly and quietly jumped in her car and lay down in the seat. Then she heard the sound of high heels coming her way, running fast. After the person passed her car, she said she sat up, and from the back, she saw a tall woman, dressed in all black from head to toe, except for her shoes.

What kind of shoes were they?

They were red in color and circled with diamonds; in fact, they were Omari's, Omari Sevens'. "The well-known designer is known for only creating and making two pairs of each shoe he designs," she said. "Two and through, nobody but you," was his motto.

"I'm sorry, but I know shoes; that's one of my weaknesses. I have over one-hundred-twenty-five pairs of shoes but no Omari Sevens'," she said.

Then she told us that it was Omari Sevens week.

My next thought was, *is the designer responsible for these murders?* But why would he be? He's a multi-millionaire with too much to lose.

Was he having affairs with these women? Was it his wife doing the killing?

All these questions were running through my head, and I'm sure they were running through Brian's too.

Immediately, I thought about Detective Brian's wife having a pair of the shoes and I wondered if she would be next.

I didn't want to say anything to him to scare him or make him think about his wife possibly having an affair, so I kept it to myself and decided to do some investigating on my own.

My first thought was to contact the designer, to see if he had any knowledge of what was going on, as I'm sure Brian was thinking about or would eventually.

Chapter 3

Omari Sevens

In my search for information, I found out that he lived in the left bank, one of the most pleasant districts in Paris.

The next day, Detective Brian called and asked me to meet him at the Sevens' home, to which I agreed.

Arriving there around 12pm, we found that Mr. Sevens was not home, but his wife Francesca was there, about to leave to go shopping. We asked if we could come in, and she agreed.

Briefly, we shared with her what was going on and our concern for her life, being his wife. She didn't seem to be bothered by it at all.

She told us that no one had contacted her or that nothing out of the ordinary had taken place, but she thanked us and told us that she would be watchful.

The detective handed her his card, instructing her to call him if she saw or heard anything.

She agreed, "I will. If I see or hear anything."

Detective Brian thanked her for her time and willingness to talk to us and we departed.

I thought about it and decided to follow her, not knowing she had called her husband to see if he could join her for lunch or that he told her he had a business meeting with a friend and he would see her later for dinner at home.

Her destination took her to the Louvre and Tuileries District, best known for the Crème de la crème designer fashions, chic home furnishings, and quality cosmetics.

As I watched her from afar, after going into two stores, I saw her staring through the window of Le Poulpry, located at 12, rue de Poitiers. The restaurant offered a delightful French dining experience.

With a 9.4 rating, it was a great choice for those seeking exquisite cuisine. The average price for a meal there is around 691m, $116.43 in American money.

Whatever it was that she saw disturbed her greatly, to the point of tears.

Me, being me, I had to know what she saw that disturbed her so much.

So, as she moved slowly from in front of the window, I eased up.

Looking through the window, I saw her husband Omari with another woman. She was dressed very nicely and simply gorgeous; but when she stood up, I saw that she was pregnant. She looked as if she was about six months, but what got me was she had on the same heels that Francesca had on.

Okay, at first glance, it could have been a client or an employee. So, what was it that disturbed Omari's wife? Was it the shoes or something else? I decided not to assume but to go in and be seated, to see if I could see or hear anything.

Wow! In about ten minutes, I saw and heard more than I cared to or expected.

This was definitely not a business meeting; this was someone he was having an affair with and she was carrying his baby.

Oh my God, no wonder Francesca walked away in tears.

It was obvious to her what it was.

To find out her husband was cheating alone was devastating, but to see that the woman he was cheating with was pregnant, giving him something she couldn't give him was too much. I knew exactly how she felt, because I, too, had experienced that hurt.

Leaving there, I immediately called Detective Brian and shared with him what I had found out. I told him how I felt Omari Sevens had lied about making only two pair of each shoe he designed and that there was definitely something to these women and these shoes.

He was in agreement with me.

I also told him that I did not believe Francesca was the one committing the murders. The look on her face was not one of anger; it was hurt, devastation and disappointment.

While sitting in my car talking to Detective Brian, I could overhear the dispatcher from his car saying that a woman had been run down by a stolen Jeep driven by a woman.

It was when the address was given that I screamed. It happened in front of Francesca's house!

Lord, please don't let it be Francesca!

Driving as fast as I could, I prayed all the way that it was not Francesca.

When I pulled up, Detective Brian had already arrived. I got out of my car to run over there, then he stopped me and told me I didn't want to see her like that.

He confirmed for me who it was.

At that point, I began to cry. Then I became very angry, thinking about him sitting there enjoying his lunch with his side chick while his wife lay dead in the street in front of their house.

I immediately called the restaurant and asked if he was still there.

The Matre'd said that he was.

"May I speak to him please? It is an emergency."

When Omari came on the phone, I identified myself to him, informing him that he needed to get home as fast as he could.

The medics worked on her for twenty minutes, but she didn't make it. Her injuries were too great.

I then walked with Detective Brian, knocking on doors to see if anybody saw anything.

Most of the neighbors were not home, but Mrs. Ramirez, who lived at the last house, answered and said that she was the one who called the police.

She stated that she was walking her dog when it happened. She said the person was driving at least eighty to ninety miles per hour, knocking Francesca so high in the air that when she came down, there was no way she could survive that.

Then she said the woman got out the car and looked at Francesca, knowing that she would not survive. She hopped back in the Jeep and drove off.

Then she said, "The crazy thing is she had on all black, from head to toe. One thing I noticed was that she had on the same shoes Francesca had on."

"Are you talking about Omari Sevens' shoes?" I asked.

"Yes, ma'am."

"How did you know?"

"Honey, I've been to their house, and Francesca showed me her shoe closet," the woman replied.

Thanking her for the information she gave us, we began to put our heads together, adding and subtracting.

About that time, Omari pulled up in a panic, barely parking the car, jumping out and running toward the ambulance.

The next thing we heard was a gut-wrenching scream coming from Omari as he found out that Francesca was dead.

A scream that told me one of two things; either in the midst of his unfaithfulness, he really loved his wife, or he was a good actor in addition to being a top shoe designer.

Brian went over to talk to him, asking me to stay over by the car. He knew I might not use good judgment at this time.

He was over there for some time.

When he returned to the car, he basically told me in short that he told Omari to handle his business concerning his wife and then come down to the police station later.

Omari was one of the best shoe designers in the world, but now he was a suspect in three murders.

We know he didn't do it, but did he hire someone else to do it? Did he stand to benefit from these deaths? How much was his wife worth dead? All these questions were running through my mind.

A couple of hours later, Omari showed up at the police station.

Brian questioned Omari for over an hour, until, finally, the questions got to him, making him angry.

He was shouting, while banging on the table, "I love my wife! I love my wife! I may have been having multiple affairs, but I loved my wife."

Affairs! I'm sure Brian heard that, too.

"If you loved her, then why all the affairs?" Brian asked him.

"Because I like a variety; plus, she couldn't give me the one thing I wanted the most. A baby."

At that point, he refused to answer any more questions without his lawyer being present.

Brian then decided to let him go, instructing him to not leave town.

I, myself, believe he was guilty of having affairs but not of murdering his wife.

Three murders and somebody was guilty, but who?

Chapter 4

Thursday

Monday, Tuesday, and Wednesday, three murders—one each day—with no arrest. So, who was the culprit, and what was their reason for all this?

Thursday night around 8pm, I got a call from Detective Brian, telling me there had been another murder. This time, it was Bre'ana, Omari's side chick.

Her friends had given her a surprise Thirsty Thursday baby shower. Upon leaving the baby shower, while she and her BFF were putting the gifts in the car, a car pulled over, a woman dressed in all black got out and started shooting, killing both of them.

Hearing the gunshots, people began to run outside as the car was speeding away.

None of the ladies who were in attendance at the baby shower saw anything because they were all still in the house cleaning up. Ambulances were called along with police.

In the meantime, some of the ladies administered CPR to both of the women, to no avail.

Even the EMS could not bring them back, not even the baby.

This was just too much!

Who was killing all these women? Who would kill a pregnant woman?

Somebody with a cold heart or no heart at all. I don't know, but I was determined to find out.

The next day was the fashion show, and I was determined to make it my business to be there.

Chapter 5

Couture Fashion Week

Couture Fashion Week was a bi-annual event held in Paris, where some of the world's most skilled artisans and fashion designers come together to showcase their bold and artful creations.

The main event was on Friday evening at 7pm.

I made sure I was there so that if there was anything to be seen, I would see it.

The haute couture collections are the pinnacle of the fashion industry, representing the ultimate in luxury and exclusivity.

The term "haute couture" comes from the French language and literally means "high sewing" or "high dress making." It was something to see. Each gown was a stunning tour de force.

When it was Omari's time to showcase his shoes, he stepped out in a black two-piece suit and a pair of black wing-tip shoes, with diamonds on the tip of the toes and diamonds on the backs of the shoes in an O. He was absolutely stunning, but how he could smile with all that was going on in his life, I'll never know. I guess at the end of the day, it's about four things, one's name, reputation, notoriety, and money.

As he stood there, posed, a woman entered, dressed in all black from head to toe, a large black hat trimmed in diamonds, and sunglasses with diamonds around the frame. The four-inch heels she had on were to die for, trimmed like the shoes Omari was wearing, with diamonds on the tip of the toes and diamonds on the backs of the shoes in an O, for Omari.

Immediately, I wondered if this could be the murderer standing right beside him.

I took plenty pictures from all angles and two videos, to share with Brian so that he could go back and show Mrs. Ramirez, who witnessed Francesca's murder and Frances Baldwin, the woman who saw the murderer in the garage.

After the show, there was a reception, and most of the models were there. I kept my eyes on one model in particular. Up close, she appeared to be six-feet tall, still walking like she was on the runway, but there was something about her that I just couldn't put my finger on.

I left before the reception was over, wanting to get my phone to Brian, so he could look at the pictures and videos I took.

"These are really good, perfect, in fact," Brian said.

He then reached out to Mrs. Ramirez and Frances Baldwin, to set a time when we could come by and show them the footage and see if they could identify the woman.

Both identified her as the killer, by her walk and the way she swayed her hands when she walked.

Upon those confirmations, Brian called Omari's secretary, to find out the name of the model and how he could get in touch with her.

We were told her name was Triniti and that she hadn't been with them long, maybe about six months.

Upon being given the address, off we went to pay Miss Triniti a visit.

Chapter 6

Triniti

Upon ringing the doorbell once, it was as if we were being expected. When the door opened and we were invited in, a man dressed in all black appeared, having the same exact outfit and shoes Omari had on the night before.

He was beautiful—not handsome, but beautiful.

Brian asked for Triniti, and the man who stood before us said, "I am she."

I know we both looked confused, but okay.

Invited to come all the way in, we went into the living room.

"Please have a seat," the beautiful man said.

Brian, cutting to the chase, informed him that the conversation would be recorded. The man said he had no problem with that.

Brian began with the questions. "So, you are Triniti?"

"Yes, I am."

"Okay, no disrespect, but are you a man or woman; what were you born as?"

"I was born a male."

"So, what is your real name?"

"It is Tristan, Tristan Cobb."

"Did you kill those women?" Brian wasted no time.

With no hesitation, the man said, "Yes."

I said to myself, *did he just admit to murder?*

Brian then asked him why.

His response was that he was trying to destroy Omari.

Before Brian could say anything else, I asked a one-word question, "Why"?

"To show him how it feels when someone you love leaves you."

He went on to explain that he and Omari were childhood friends, brought up in a foster home together. He explained that several times, he had to defend Omari because of bullying and how he was picked on because of his looks.

"He was called a girl, a fag, and a sissy, because he was handsome and talented. He had dreams then of being a fashion designer and would share them with us. The other boys would tease him, but I would always listen to him and encourage him. If they tried to fight him, I would always take up for him.

They no longer bothered me because I had already proven that I wasn't weak. I would fight and win, thanks to having been taught karate by the neighbor who lived next door."

He paused a moment and then continued, "We both were artists. He would design clothes, especially shoes for women, and I loved to paint. We had made a pact that if one of us made it, the other would make it too, but Omari didn't keep his promise. He forgot all about me."

Another pause and then, "There was a new kid who came to the home and thought he could bully us.

I ended up beating him within an inch of his life. Because of that, I was put in juvenile detention. In there, having to defend myself for various reasons, I ended beating someone else within an inch of their life, but that incident got me a five-year prison sentence."

We listened as he told the rest of his story. "In there, I was gang raped, contracted AIDS, and now, I have a death sentence. Then upon being released, I had nowhere to go and became homeless. At that point, I no longer cared. Again, I tried everything to reach out to Omari, but to no avail. I tried contacting the magazines I would see him in and on the front of, but nobody would help me. At that point, I became determined to find him at all costs. I had nothing to lose."

Tristan looked at us for a moment, silent, before going on. "I said to myself every day, 'Vengeance is mine and I will repay!' It took me a while to get enough money to get here, and the things I had to do to get it, I don't even care to mention. Countless times, I tried to reach out to him, but to no avail. I was ignored, so I came up with a plan to destroy him and make him hurt the way I did; then, in the end, kill him as well as myself. At least we would be together again."

Looking over to the side of the chair I was sitting in, I saw a portrait of Omari and asked if he painted it. He nodded yes. It was absolutely spellbinding; he was really gifted.

Triniti continued, "So, that's why I murdered those women. I wanted him to hurt like I have hurt for years. I wanted him to be blamed for the murders and go to prison like I did. Since he was only questioned and not arrested, I had planned to kill him today, as well as myself."

Brian and I both sat there in wonder that he would say something like that with such boldness.

Two questions from me were, "How did you start modeling for him? How did he not recognize you?"

Answering the second question first, he said, "Because I always dressed as a woman, wore sunglasses, changed my voice when I was around him. Plus, I am a professional makeup artist. One day, I was told by one of the customers at the restaurant where I worked that this agency was looking for new models and that I should go and audition. Only, I went as a woman, not a man, and was hired on the spot. I had practiced for years how to walk a runway."

He went on to say, "At the audition, one of the things I mentioned to the lady I was auditioning for was that I never take my glasses off for anybody. I told them that was my signature, my mystery, keeping the audience curious about who I really was. She said that was fine, and I was in."

He laughed. "Then when they saw me walk the runway and do my signature turn, they really no longer cared about the glasses. Omari said he would make sure I had glasses to go with every outfit I wore."

At that point, Tristan handed us a letter to give to Omari; he promised that it was not laced with anything, just apologizing for what he had done and telling him how much he loved him as a brother.

What I couldn't understand was now that he was here and in there, a part of the agency, why didn't he just reveal himself to Omari?

The last thing he asked was if we would give the portrait he had painted to Omari along with a letter.

What I didn't see when looking at the portrait the first time was how he had signed the portrait in the bottom, right-hand corner, *"Brothers 4 Life."*

As Brian asked him to stand so he could put the cuffs on him, he began to convulse.

What was happening?

We immediately thought he was having a seizure, but, in fact, he was overdosing.

Brian called for an ambulance while I started CPR, but to no avail, and by the time the ambulance arrived, he was dead.

What was going on? What did he take?

Later, I discovered he had taken enough fentanyl to kill an elephant.

After everything and everybody had cleared, we went to share the news with Omari.

We shared with him our findings, telling him that it was an old friend of his who committed the murders, with a plan to kill him next.

Handing him the letter that Tristan gave us to give to him, I can honestly say that I have never seen a man cry with such intensity.

We don't know what the letter said, but whatever it was, it made him cry even harder. At that point, he got up and went to retrieve a box filled with letters that he had sent to Tristan over the years, stamped

Return to Sender. His plan was to give them to Tristan when he found him, no matter how long it took; he had faith that they would reunite someday somehow.

Omari had no idea that Tristan had changed his name to Triniti after being released from prison.

The point being, he had not forgotten about Tristan, and if he would have just made himself known to him, everything would have worked out and two friends would have been reunited.

Maybe Triniti felt that Omari would not have accepted him being gay, I don't know, but he wanted to make

Omari feel the loneliness and hurt that he had felt over the years.

If you ask me, I believe that if he had just told Omari who he was when he arrived, they could have picked up where they left off.

As I conclude this story, I'm sure you're wondering why the detective's wife was not among those murdered.

Well, it's because the shoes she had were knock offs and she was faithful to her husband!

BAM!

About the Author

Dr. Ruth Wilson

A native of Louisville, Kentucky, Dr. Ruth Wilson is a dynamic force of faith, wisdom, and community transformation. As a devoted mother, proud grandmother and great grandmother, she brings warmth, courage and strength to every role she inhabits—whether in the pulpit, the classroom, or the heart of her neighborhood.

A seasoned pastor, gifted teacher, and prophetic voice, Dr. Wilson has spent decades uplifting others through spiritual guidance and tireless activism. Her leadership has sparked change across generations, making her a respected pillar in both religious and civic circles.

She is the celebrated author of eight inspiring books and the visionary playwright behind one powerful stage production, each work reflecting her passion for healing, empowerment, and truth. Whether mentoring youth, advocating for justice, or preaching with fire and grace, Dr. Wilson continues to shape lives with purpose and compassion.

Her legacy is one of bold faith, unwavering service, and a commitment to building bridges where others see walls.

More Books by Dr. Ruth Wilson

HOW TO **PROPERLY** talk to **GOD**

DR.RUTH WILSON

IT WILL FIND YOU

DR. RUTH WILSON

DO YOU HAVE IT

?

DR. RUTH WILSON